TRUMP
SONNETS

Volume 7
His Further Virus Monologues

Ken Waldman

TRUMP SONNETS

Volume 7

His Further Virus Monologues

Ken Waldman

Ridgeway Press
Roseville, Michigan

Book Design: Jerry Hagins

Ridgeway Press
P.O. Box 120
Roseville, Michigan 48066

1 2 3 4 5 6 7 8 9 10

Acknowledgments:
　　After the writing of this long poem, and the
continuing support of Ridgeway Press, this book came
to be because of the support of family, friends, and
readers. I specifically want to thank Hal & Lisa Tovin,
Lizzie Thompson, Paul Fericano, Sunil Freeman, Mark
Tamsula & Barbara Rosner, Robert Baird, Jerry Hagins
& Beth Chrisman, Stephen Sunderlin, Suzanne Todd,
Tom Wayne & Will Leathem of Prospero's Books,
Ricklen Nobis, Juan Romano, Elizabeth English,
Charlie Carew & Rachael Fulbright, Mike Branch,
Jared Yates Sexton, Maria Nazos, Mike Shay, Jane
Varley, Jim Clark, Bob Cooperman.
　　I also want to directly thank M.L. Liebler, the
publisher of this book, and the prior six in this series.
　　Thanks, too, to the bookstores and readers that
greeted the earlier *Trump Sonnets* books. Also, thanks
to the Puffin Foundation, whose grant for the theater
piece associated with this project, *Trump Sonnets or:
How I've Taken on Donald Trump (and Won)*, came at
a crucial time. Without such support, *Volume 7*
wouldn't have come to be.

Contents

I

July 1, 2020 2
July 2, 2020 3
July 3, 2020 4
July 4, 2020 5
July 5, 2020 6
July 6, 2020 7
July 7, 2020 8
July 8, 2020 9
July 9, 2020 10
July 10, 2020 11
July 11, 2020 12
July 12, 2020 13
July 13, 2020 14
July 14, 2020 15
July 15, 2020 16
July 16, 2020 17
July 17, 2020 18
July 18, 2020 19
July 19, 2020 20
July 20, 2020 21
July 21, 2020 22
July 22, 2020 23
July 23, 2020 24
July 24, 2020 25
July 25, 2020 26
July 26, 2020 27
July 27, 2020 28
July 28, 2020 29
July 29, 2020 30
July 30, 2020 31
July 31, 2020 32

II

August 1, 2020 34
August 2, 2020 35
August 3, 2020 36
August 4, 2020 37
August 5, 2020 38
August 6, 2020 39
August 7, 2020 40

August 8, 2020 41
August 9, 2020 42
August 10, 2020 43
August 11, 2020 44
August 12, 2020 45
August 13, 2020 46
August 14, 2020 47
August 15, 2020 48
August 16, 2020 49
August 17, 2020 50
August 18, 2020 51
August 19, 2020 52
August 20, 2020 53
August 21, 2020 54
August 22, 2020 55
August 23, 2020 56
August 24, 2020 57
August 25, 2020 58
August 26, 2020 59
August 27, 2020 60
August 28, 2020 61
August 29, 2020 62
August 30, 2020 63
August 31, 2020 64

III

September 1, 2020 66
September 2, 2020 67
September 3, 2020 68
September 4, 2020 69
September 5, 2020 70
September 6, 2020 71
September 7, 2020 72

Postscript

September 11, 2020 74
September 14, 2020 75
September 20, 2020 76
September 24, 2020 77
September 30, 2020 78

I

July 1, 2020

I don't fear a thing, and I'm not afraid
of the Chinese flu. They're very evil,
the Democrats. The very worst people
in the world. They wear masks. They haven't made
money like I have. Their blacks haven't paid
taxes for years. They're so incredible,
these Democratic lowlifes. Unstable
protesters hate the old statues. I've said
we can't let them do this. The Democrats
loot, cheat, deface federal property
for no good reason. I treat them like rats,
which is what they deserve. They play dirty,
the lefty socialists. I'm very clean.
The cleanest! Trump Hotels — perfectly clean!

July 2, 2020

The virus hasn't left yet, but it will,
and when it goes it will be like magic,
and all will be fine. What's really tragic
is the decision with the book. We'll kill
publication—my lawyers say so. Bill
Barr tells me my niece can't write it. He'll fix
this in the next weeks. No one's getting sick—
and infections are way down. A new pill,
my Trump Vaccine, will be ready real soon
according to my sources. We can't wait—
I've demanded a taste this afternoon.
We'll fully reopen next month. A great
month, August. Hot! Less than a million dead—
much less. A beautiful number of dead.

July 3, 2020

All my life I've wanted a Mount Trumpmore,
but mostly I didn't know it. My face
alone in rock really high up some place
near one of my golf clubs. I'd like wide doors
at the bottom to fit more visitors
who'll climb inside stairs to the top. Quick pace
and you're done in two hours. In most cases
very long lines. Huge parking lot and store.
Huge tour buses. My Mount Trumpmore will be
the seventh wonder of the modern world,
like a brand new Statue of Liberty
and Mount Rushmore rolled into one. A world-
renowned monument. My South Dakota
rallies are great. I love South Dakota.

July 4, 2020

This is my favorite day of the year.
I love birthdays and I love my country
more than anyone. With so much money,
I run the White House like a business. We're
keeping our America great, so fear
nothing! We're winning! The flu probably
will leave this week or next. We have to see
because it's a big monkey that appears
and then disappears. It doesn't matter
how we kill it, but we will because that's
our country's tremendous way. I'd rather
do it immediately. Democrats
choose death since they don't love America
or the flag. July 4th! America!

July 5, 2020

Why won't the loser mainstream media
leave me and my family alone? Fake
news, people. Fake news! All they do is make
themselves look stupid. They have no idea
what we accomplished in South Dakota,
Arizona, here in D.C.. We'll take
charge the next four months, and I hope it breaks
his heart, Mr. No-Talent Obama,
who everyone knows was the very worst
in history. How the lamestream loves to
prop him way up because he was the first
of his race. He's behind every statue
that goes down. That makes him a real traitor,
and we'll treat him accordingly. Traitor!

July 6, 2020

Obama and Old Sleepy Joe Biden
are in this together. That's obvious
from the start. They've been the most dangerous
duo this country's ever seen. Inside
their White House—such stories. They're still hiding
those crimes and will commit more. Serious
crimes. Traitors! That's because they both hate us,
real Americans, who are now fighting
for law and order. They'll fire the police
everywhere. Old Sleepy Joe Biden will
follow his master, Obama. That's twice
the damage we're looking at. Puppet! We'll
never recover if he's president—
the new Obama. I'm your president!

July 7, 2020

Three and a half years and I'm looking back,
and looking forward. We're in big crisis —
radical Democrats have wanted this
and they own it. They've wanted to attack
our way of life. They pull strings so the blacks
are on the streets. It's a dirty business,
this racket of theirs. How they'd love to kiss
our great country good-bye. They're maniacs,
from top to bottom. Why we've let traitors
in government, I'll never know. The swamp
is deep and wide, and full of the worst haters
I've ever seen. It's the enemy camp
right here in the open. The Democrats
are trouble. We must wipe out Democrats.

July 8, 2020

I can't believe it. There's no other niece
like this in history. We'll have to sue
and destroy every book. No one can do
this to me and my family. A beast,
she's a beast. Illegal books! The police
will be getting involved here. She's not who
she says she is. All lies! None of it's true—
not a single word. Why can't I have peace
to do my job? The greatest president
can't be treated like this. The niece is sick
and we'll jail her. She was an accident,
according to my failed brother. Wicked,
nasty know-nothing—she's not family.
I have the most wonderful family.

July 9, 2020

Huge Democratic plot with the Chinese
and their flu has gone totally global—
damages to our economy will
be written in history. This disease
is the Democrats' plan—they're starved to seize
power any way possible. They'll kill
millions to do it. It's incredible
how corrupt they are. Along with Chinese
operatives, they'll rig the election—
that's next on their list. They got to the niece
and you've seen what happened. Have I mentioned
her book is full of lies? What a dumb piece
of work. The lefty Democrats brainwashed
her in school. Schools are corrupt. They brainwash.

July 10, 2020

Yesterday was the most terrible day
of this awful year. I hate the Supreme
Court when they decide to quit on my team,
which is a mistake. My lawyers have ways
to reverse this. As president, I say
what laws really mean. It's my oldest dream
to have a perfect job like this—I seem
to do it perfectly. Why can't we pray
they come up with a better decision?
All I want to do is get on the course
and play eighteen holes. This next election
will be my salvation. No one can force
me to do anything. I'm president,
and I intend to remain president.

July 11, 2020

The least I could do was commute my pal
Roger's very unfair sentence. This way
important justice has been served. He's paid
a big price, same as me. They are so foul,
the Pelosi Democrats. Some wear towels
on their heads. And masks all day, every day.
I'm so sick and tired of it. If I play
a round of golf, or help a friend, they howl
like I've killed someone. There's no Benghazi
here. The worst thing has been this Chinese flu,
but deaths are going down. In weeks we'll see
this invisible germ disappear. Who
would have thought I'd do so perfectly well
curing people? My good friend, Roger, is well.

July 12, 2020

The job of being president is not
for everybody. There are days I want
to leave and not come back here, but I can't
because presidents can't do that. A lot
of bravery to be me when I've got
the fake lamestream to deal with. I just want
to be treated fairly. Instead they hunt
me like an animal. It's nasty — not
fair at all. I stayed in the White House — please
know I was stuck inside for months — and worked
harder than anyone. Dr. Fauci
was amazed, but then he became a jerk
and tried to shut the whole country down for good.
I stopped him! I did very, very good!

July 13, 2020

I can't believe they're fighting us on schools
opening. What's wrong with everybody?
Why don't they want our great economy
back? The Chinese flu? That's a lot of bull
as far as I'm concerned. We need a full
work force, which means that schools have got to be
ready to go. Students, teachers, staff—we've
got to be on the same page. They're such fools,
the teachers and parents who are negative
on the subject. Kids want to see their friends
and play sports. They're young and brave. They'll all live
even if they get infected. I'll send
Barron to school. Melania and I do
what all good patriotic parents do.

July 14, 2020

No one understands me. I work such long
hours and hardly ever sleep. The virus
made a mess of the world. Being famous
is not always a reward. They're so wrong
about me — I'm on the phone acting strong
with fellow leaders. No one can stop us.
Such intelligence, and I'm the genius
among them. I'm not just playing ping-pong
here — this is much bigger than golf even,
what I've done for the country. And no one
seems to care. I should be getting seven
or eight global awards. I'm on the phone
massively saving lives around the clock,
except when I watch Sean at 9 o'clock.

July 15, 2020

I'm happy to have made sure Jeff Sessions
lost in Alabama. He's a traitor
and loser. That's what happens to traitors,
and I can't wait for these next elections
and my next four years. All televisions
everywhere on OAN. And later
at night on Fox for Sean. I'm creator
of the greatest ratings in television
history. I'll see that Democratic
traitors like Obama, Old Sleepy Joe
Biden, Pelosi, Schiff taste my magic
and get locked in prison for life. Also
we'll round up possibly the worst traitor,
Sessions. He's the Republican traitor.

July 16, 2020

I won't read unfair polls. I'm confident,
like I was confident four years ago.
I've no fear at all of Old Sleepy Joe,
who takes orders from Obama. He's meant
to stay ex-vice president, lieutenant
to the most corrupt in history. No
one who knows him will vote for him. He shows
no leadership or strength from his basement
hideout. It's sad how he runs a loser
campaign and thinks he has people's votes.
Liar! I'll say it again. A loser
Democrat. You'll see. I'll get twice his votes—
election night I'll be declared winner
by landslide. America loves winners.

July 17, 2020

Why doesn't everyone see what I see:
the greatest leader in the history
of our country. I tell you, the Chinese
flu has been exactly like my mighty
TV show. Lots of action. It's made me
the biggest star ever because I see
all the most important details. Funny
how real life has been so much like TV,
and here I am making the Chinese flu
go away. So many tests! The most tests
in the world. Nobody does what I do,
and I keep outdoing myself. The best
president in history. Our country
is the greatest. I've become our country.

July 18, 2020

Only I can solve the infrastructure
which has been ignored for many decades.
Roads haven't been built. People are afraid
to cross bridges. Most cities are sewers
of dark crime. By modernizing we'll cure
the worst problems in our country. I've stayed
true to my promises — I promise great
improvements. What a tremendous future
for all of us. Old Sleepy Joe only
wants to follow his master, Obama,
which means failure. He's a sad and lonely
man, a career Democrat. The drama
he'd cause — he'd lead us into civil war.
He'd take your guns. Old Sleepy Joe means war.

July 19, 2020

Kidnapping? What are they talking about?
I know there are some very bad people
on the streets. They loot and do terrible
things to buildings and statues. There's no doubt
they hate America and are without
shame for their criminal acts. Horrible,
horrible people. I don't know what we'll
do with them. I'll leave that to others out
in the field who are observing first-hand
the many unlawful acts. The West Coast,
I've got to hand it to them. Take Portland,
Seattle, Los Angeles, the three most
dangerous cities in the world. I'm up
for four more years. We'll lock protesters up.

July 20, 2020

Why would I promise to accept results
of an election that hasn't happened?
I'm certain to win. That's what I do when
I want something — I win. It's an insult
to think otherwise. The liberal cult
of Democrats are such losers. They tend
to lie and cheat. They'll commit fraud and bend
rules. No more mail-in voting! That's the fault
of post offices, which we're closing down
to make more efficient and save money.
How Obama ran us into the ground —
Old Sleepy Joe would sink us lower. See,
Obama is his master. The Deep State
traitors want control. I'm saving the States.

July 21, 2020

I did great on the diagnostic tests,
which were hard. I pointed out elephant,
and they didn't ask but I always want
french fries with my hamburgers. I'm the best
president ever. Absolute greatest
man on earth. I love being president
because I can always do what I want,
which is part of the job. I'm making guests
at all my hotels and clubs pay double,
but soon it will be up to triple. I aced
those tests. Everyone else would have trouble
with those hard questions, but not me. In case
you're wondering, I want a hamburger
with french fries tonight. A big hamburger!

July 22, 2020

Very, very bad people on the streets
of cities. They call themselves Antifa —
they're terrorists who hate America,
and invite all migrants to join them. Treat
them all like dogs! Round them up! We'll defeat
them like the Chinese flu. It's a good idea,
making them disappear. We'll crush Antifa
like bugs. When they're gone, we'll be safe to greet
the new day this November. I can't wait
to show how everyone's completely wrong
again. Jailing Antifa keeps us great.
We'll also break the Deep State before long.
We've got the worst people on city streets.
We have to make it safe to walk the streets.

July 23, 2020

The radical left is the biggest threat
to our great nation. There's Old Sleepy Joe,
his master, Obama, and we all know
Crazy Nancy, AOC, and their set
of Deep State hoodlums. They want us in debt
as they let in all the Muslims. I have no
doubt they'd fire police, take away guns, go
shut down all the beautiful churches, get
their radical menu front and center.
They're all un-American and ugly.
What kind of country is this? We enter
a critical time. I'm democracy.
I'm an American who's against hate.
Their radical policies support hate.

July 24, 2020

Don't ever listen to the doomsayers
except to tell them they can go to hell.
Everything is beautiful, beautiful
except for the Deep Staters and their layers
of corruption and lamestream news. Unfair
what I've faced. Old Sleepy Joe looks unwell—
he's been in his basement for months—so tell
me why they don't mention *that*. They don't care
if he's dead as long as they have their polls—
which I don't believe for a split second.
I know when I walk off the eighteenth hole
on November 3rd, I'm second to none.
I'm very prepared for my second term.
No president's done more in his first term.

July 25, 2020

You've got to understand they're really sick,
the Democratic Party. AOC,
or whatever her name, is as nasty
a woman as I've ever seen. Wicked
witch from Puerto Rico. She hates us. *Kick
her out*, I tell ICE. But in this country
for now she's free to bitch. I guarantee
she'll end up locked away in an attic
somewhere, babbling lies, at least out of sight.
She thinks her very bad New York looters
are hungry and blames protests on some rights
no one's ever heard of. We have shooters
aiming at all those Portland protesters
who'll wreck our country. Arrest protesters!

July 26, 2020

Person, woman, man, camera, TV—
a week later, I still have the words. Who
knew I'd score above genius? My IQ
is incredible. This isn't easy—
Old Sleepy Joe wouldn't even agree
to take this test. He can't even tell blue
from red, which was a simpler question. True
enough, my remarkable memory
is in great shape. I recited all five
in perfect order so got extra points.
Unlike Old Sleepy Joe, I'm still alive—
I do tests and play golf. He's got bad joints.
I'll say it here like I did on TV:
Person, woman, man, camera, TV.

July 27, 2020

No one's taken this more seriously
than me. From the beginning I stopped planes
from China, home of the flu, and the main
threat to health. You can ask Dr. Fauci,
who by the way made mistakes. We've maybe
saved a million lives so far. The best brains,
most of all mine, are hard at work. We've drained
the swamp at CDC. Our briefings see
huge ratings—better than The Super Bowl.
Sports have returned. Golf. Baseball. The bubble
allows for basketball. Expect the whole
economy back in time for the schools
next month. I'm so proud of what I've done here.
The most tests in the world—didn't you hear?

July 28, 2020

Dr. Fauci has no business throwing
a first pitch. That's the work of presidents.
When I was a boy, I'd swing for the fence,
and my meanest fastball stung. That's knowing
the sport. I don't like what Fauci's doing,
stealing my job. He's much worse than Mike Pence
sometimes. At least the Yankees have the sense
to ask me to take the mound. No screwing
with a popular president! Too bad
I'll be busy with the Chinese virus,
so can't make the game. It's wrong Fauci had
time—he should be working. It's serious
stuff, this unseen enemy. I'm busy
making so many policies. Busy!

July 29, 2020

All they know to do is conduct witch hunts.
Bill Barr isn't perfect, but he's better
than Jeff Sessions. They're all in the gutter,
nasty House Democrats. Questions! Witch hunt!
This shouldn't be happening. It doesn't
make sense, and next term I'll write a letter
banning Democrat-run panels, whether
they like it or not. They're a sad comment
on our great country. They don't understand
the point. Who do they think they are, going
on TV? A lynch mob! I have to hand
it to them though — I've watched their showboating
and dopey stupidity. The Senate
is a smarter bunch. I love the Senate.

July 30, 2020

Every step I've had it under control,
this horrifying Chinese virus. No
one could have done more. Dr. Fauci knows,
and so does Dr. Birx, how it's hit whole
countries quickly. No one sees it! I told
Mike Pence he'd be in charge so we could show
the world how we beat invisible foes
because that's America. I bet Old
Sleepy Joe would do a hundred times worse
because he's locked in a basement. Lots more
would have died. Lots more infections. A worse
economy with Old Sleepy Joe. Stores
are open everywhere now. Baseball, too.
We're doing great reopening schools, too.

July 31, 2020

I know we can't move this year's election.
I was only joking while wondering
if such a thing was possible. Nothing
replaces our mighty Constitution.
I love our great Second Amendment—guns
always have a place here. What's occurring
this year has never happened. We're funding
so many lost jobs. This year's election
can't be moved, but someone said we can save
lots of money by moving the date back,
and making more safe choices. It's a brave
idea we can think about. I'm on track
for a vaccine that will change everything.
Mail-in voting just corrupts everything.

II

August 1, 2020

As president I can have generals
do my business. They follow all orders,
and I'm Commander in Chief. My orders
are always perfect. I've led successful
foreign raids. Now we're fighting criminal
protesters in failing cities. Borders
are not secure — I'm only a quarter
through doing my job here. The generals
are there to see I'll still be president
in my eighties. Four more years. Then four more,
and I hope more. Great countries don't prevent
their greatest men from staying in power.
I'm the best ever Commander in Chief.
Generals follow orders from their chief.

August 2, 2020

I promise the virus will disappear
suddenly as it came. I never said when,
which means I'm correct. Georgia, Maryland,
Florida, Texas, it will disappear
and finally leave us alone. Let's be clear —
you'll see it vanish. I'll be right again
just like I always am. So visit friends,
go shop, eat out, and travel without fear.
The economy will bounce back and stocks
will climb to new heights. I promise all that
and much more. I'll also make sure that Fox
News returns to glory and Democrats
will be put on trial for their many crimes.
We'll start with Obama, the head of crimes.

August 3, 2020

An absentee ballot isn't the same
as mail-in. That's what's wrong with the fake news —
their inaccurate polls want me to lose
in November. The lamestream will be lame —
that's who they are. It's their favorite game,
blaming Trump. What they say is so untrue
and unfair. They have no actual clue
what's going on here. It's really a shame
because the enthusiasm for me
is incredible. No one can believe how
popular I've made the presidency —
must-see TV. For most states we allow
absentee votes and encourage those in
that predicament. We're suing mail-ins.

August 4, 2020

We're doing tremendous in the key states
of Florida, Wisconsin, Ohio,
Pennsylvania, Carolina. I know
how the sad, failing lamestream operates —
it's all fake news death numbers. How they hate
me and America. If you follow
their polls, you'd think I lost last time. I do
what no one does, which is why I create
enthusiasm never before seen.
The suburbs always decide last minute,
which will swing things my way. I've never been
a bit afraid of Old Sleepy Joe. It
will be a glorious Trump landslide.
Senate Republicans? One more landslide.

August 5, 2020

Leagues are playing baseball and basketball,
just like I proposed. As we reopen
all of our public schools, we'll have to cope
with the Chinese flu. I know it's a tall
order, but just as we build border walls,
we can do this too. So much got broken
by this plague, but I have tremendous hope
that stocks will rise higher than ever. All
it takes is children in schools, their parents
at work, unemployment back to record
lows. What I say is the best common sense
ever. I know what experts don't. I've heard
people say I should get the Nobel Prize.
Most tests, and least dead: that's worth a big prize.

August 6, 2020

Why is everybody so negative
to me and my whole family? Frankly,
it's probably why we have so many
infections from the Chinese virus. Give
us a chance. People forget that they live
in the greatest country in history.
Compare us to anywhere: Italy,
Brazil, Spain, China—and I'm positive
they'd rather live here. We're continuing
to test more. More tests equals more cases,
which is obvious, and why we're suing
the fake *New York Times*. Just watch the faces
when we win in court. Our schools are the best
and I'm proud to open them. I'm the best.

August 7, 2020

I know many things I can't talk about,
but we have a number of surprises
for October. Really big surprises
I wish I could tell you. First, there's no doubt
I'll be re-elected. I'm not without
the smartest people. We're early-risers
and work around the clock to beat the liars
who invent fake news. I've figured it out,
and wish I could tell you the huge secrets
we have planned. All I can say is *Watch out
for Donald Trump!* He's going to win it
all again. I'm excited. No amount
of nasty godless ones will hold us back.
I know so much. I'll certainly be back.

August 8, 2020

I've learned I can do briefings anywhere
and announce them just before. In some ways
it's much easier, though I have to stay
ready for the cameras. It's unfair
I can't do as many rallies. I swear
Crazy Nancy and Obama must pay
for what they're doing. Every single day
they're killing Americans, and they dare
to criticize me. Then there's their puppet,
Old Sleepy Joe, sitting in his basement,
doing who knows what. He hates all of it—
God, religion, guns. There's no argument
from him. No nothing. Just dopey basement
broadcasts. I'm the best. I have no basement.

August 9, 2020

He's remarkable, the new postmaster
general. Great businessman. A great guy
and quite a donor. Whatever he'll try,
he'll end on top. It's been a disaster
there for years. He says mail's moving faster
and at less cost. No one wants to know why
the post office loses billions — they're sly
with the racket. At last a manager
there I can trust. The post office is sick
and has been very sick for many years.
My postmaster is making crucial, quick
improvements for this November. I hear
the Democrats want to sue. Lots of luck
with that. I own the courts. I make my luck.

August 10, 2020

I know what I'm supposed to do today.
Dr. Fauci is making me nervous.
We can't have him talking about crisis
after crisis. It will all be okay
soon, real soon. We know it's going away
just like it's doing elsewhere. Some of us,
like me, know as much about this business
as a doctor like Fauci. It's always
that way. Maybe I'll have Mike Pence fire him,
though I think it's better to wait until
after the election. The big problem
is all the tests. It's all those tests that kill
and infect. That's one reason for my tweets
these days. Too many tests. Not enough tweets.

August 11, 2020

I continue to do a perfect job
as the Democrats and Republicans
fight in House and Senate. I'm not a fan
of this government. What they do is rob
and cheat. Washington's just a giant mob
of traitors. You can't trust man or woman—
they stab from behind. But I'm smart and can
beat them at their game. It's levers and knobs—
I'll go on TV, send another tweet,
threaten budget cuts, close beautiful deals.
Loyal Americans happily greet
my words. They hate how the Democrats steal,
and how some Republicans clash with me.
I'm running this country perfectly. Me!

August 12, 2020

Old Sleepy Joe had to choose a nasty
California senator. Out of touch,
he's so out of touch. I've never seen such
a corrupt bunch. Senile old man and brassy
female. An unpresidential crazy
pairing. Just look at them. Could they be much
different? Unpleasant sight. They're not church
people either. Old Sleepy is lazy
and she's crabby. If she's American,
you could fool me. I've heard lots of stories
about her. Mean and nasty! A chicken
and a turkey. Socialists don't worry
me — they're radicals who don't have a chance.
I'm keeping us great. I like my chances.

August 13, 2020

Old Sleepy Joe is so senile and sad —
it's a lot to think he'll still be with us
next year. He's not healthy. If the virus
from China doesn't find him, he'll be glad
to sit in his basement. He's never had
this kind of pressure. It's a serious
job, the presidency. It's obvious
his vice president pick is very bad
for many reasons. She's a liberal
socialist, even worse than Obama
if that's possible. Extreme radical
and maybe she was born in Jamaica,
so she's not African American
as claimed. Phony! I'm the American!

August 14, 2020

It's ridiculous the post office spends
billions yet it's not even up to speed.
Money we lose there is better needed
for Chinese flu vaccines and for defense
against terrorists. Besides, no one sends
letters these days, which means they can't compete
with FedEx or UPS—they've cheated
our country for years. How bad? It depends
on how close you look. Who wants a corrupt
election that's not decided for months?
This mail-in voting, I'm leaving it up
to the courts. No law says we have to fund
an inferior service. They've lost their way.
I'm the boss so we're doing this my way.

August 15, 2020

Old Sleepy Joe and his shady master,
Obama, chose an angry, horrible
female for their team. She's truly awful—
where do they find these walking disasters?
A nasty California senator
from Jamaica. It's very probable
she's illegal. It's even possible
she was born in India. I've passed her
case to the DOJ. They think she's lied
about her whole family history
plus is hiding lots. We have to decide
how far to investigate her story.
Look at her! A dishonest madwoman.
I enjoy a different type of woman.

August 16, 2020

We've made excellent progress with China,
Russia, everywhere in the world. Respect
for our long-time leadership had been wrecked
by Obama. Our great America
was laughed at by all of them: Canada,
Mexico, Germany, France. Just inspect
the unfair treaties. I knew what was next—
more Muslims coming from Somalia,
Yemen, Syria. They don't stop coming,
and caravans up from El Salvador,
Guatemala, Honduras. It's something,
building a wall, signing orders, all for
the protection of our beautiful land
and people. I'm loved all over this land!

August 17, 2020

It's a very sad day. My brother died,
and we were very close. I don't know why
my family has suffered so. The lies
people always tell. My niece has no pride.
Horrible girl. My younger brother tried
to stop her, and now he's dead. All the lies—
they never stop. If one of my kids buys
a house, or takes a trip, you'd think they spied
for Russia. It's Old Sleepy Joe who's paid
by China along with his boy. His pick
for vice president, I hear she's afraid
we'll find she's illegal. She's a tragic
figure, right with Obama. Look at them.
It's a very sad day, but we'll beat them.

August 18, 2020

Why should I care about the post office?
I can't remember when I last used one.
What's important is our Constitution,
which I love, as does my talented vice
president, Mike Pence. So I've put a price
on the post office so we can bargain
with the loser Democrats. Let them fund
my budget; then they'll have their post office.
There's no one who strikes more and better deals
than me. You have to be tough to get what
you want. When it comes to business, I'm real,
which means I can beat leftist Democrats.
No one I know goes in a post office.
Pay me, and they'll have their post office.

August 19, 2020

Unfair so much boring television
with speeches no one wants to see or hear.
Lots of older women, black people, queers,
radical leftist un-American
socialists. It's a freak show convention
that I should stop from airing. It's too near
my keynotes next week which will strike huge fear
in the liberals' hearts. Watch me mention
my plans to save the failing post office
from extinction. A hero president
can do that. Old Sleepy Joe isn't nice,
and the black Asian is an accident
waiting to happen. Things are bad, people.
We Republicans have the best people.

August 20, 2020

The Democrats shouldn't play politics
next week during our convention. Unfair,
and I'm about to file suit. They don't care
about democracy. I'd love to fix
this giant problem. No hearings! I'm sick
of their witch hunts and hoaxes. They're prepared
to lie and waste everyone's time. I've shared
this with staff. They're such a terrible mix
of people, the Democrats, so next term
we'll remove them from chairing committees.
I promise success since I can confirm
lots more good judges. Everyone agrees
radical Democrats shouldn't govern.
I'm the one who knows best how to govern.

August 21, 2020

This Democratic week has been the worst—
it shouldn't be legal to do all this.
I'm president. They can't make their business
public like that. No one cares. I'm the first
to understand that. We have to reverse
all their garbage next week. MAGA misses
me. I've heard QAnon loves me. This is
what I mean. Good people. The best. The worst
have been on TV. Speeches have been awful.
Obama. His loud wife. Pocahontas
made an appearance. So many total
lies about me. It was complete chaos.
Next week I'll have my way and show the world
the true direction of our brave, new world.

August 22, 2020

I heard the news and it's unfortunate
about Steve Bannon. There were times we spoke,
but it was long ago. They say he broke
laws, but I don't know a thing. The private
wall was a very bad idea. A great
monument, our border wall. It's a hoax
that it's got problems. The Democrats poke
where they shouldn't. There's a lot on our plates —
Steve worked for me at one time, and I wish
him well, but I know nothing about his
side projects. Doing business is vicious —
winners and losers. You can swing and miss.
Steven Bannon is a very good guy.
Smart, too. But, no, I hardly know the guy.

August 23, 2020

What they're doing to Postmaster DeJoy
is criminal. I didn't appoint him.
I don't know him, so what's the big problem?
One more Democratic hoax! They enjoy
their hearings because there's no other joy
in their lives. Losers! That's what's wrong with them.
The mail still goes. They want socialism
forever. Losers! They want to destroy
America, and now they're taking aim
on who I hear is a patriotic man
doing a very fine job. It's the same
post office that's failing for years. I stand
for action and success. I'm a winner!
Postmasters have hard jobs. I'm a winner!

August 24, 2020

Today my party's great convention starts—
it's what the most people are waiting for.
Last week's was a bad joke. We'll have much more
excitement. Tonight I think the best part
will be my announcement of a target
date for a Chinese flu vaccine. The poor
Democrats won't admit by October
we'll have a cure. I've gotten to the heart
and I promise in two short months
we will fully open the whole country.
They said it couldn't be done. Two short months
and we'll celebrate an economy
like no other. It's unbelievable
how I've succeeded. Unbelievable!

August 25, 2020

Four more years, eight more years, sixteen more years—
that's the hope of loyal Americans.
We've gathered among our favorite friends
to honor just like we honored four years
ago. This has been a time we've faced fears
larger than any ever known. Sudden
virus, economic downturn, black men
demanding the right to roam and loot. Hear
what I have to say: I'm only getting
started. Another term at the White House,
where I'm standing now, would be a great thing,
a beautiful thing. I love the White House,
and have made it home. Melania, too.
We'll stay here forever. Ivanka, too.

August 26, 2020

It's tremendous how my great convention
is going. Very fine speeches by such
remarkable talents. How I've been touched,
and then I speak. Every night I mention
what I've done and what has my attention.
The future is critical. There's so much
still to accomplish. I have the best bunch
in the Cabinet now. Steve Mnuchin
has done a wonderful job with money
despite the horrific Chinese virus.
By the way, watch how the economy
rebounds in the next weeks. I've gotten us
a vaccine even if the Deep State hates
the truth. Donald Trump is for love, not hate.

August 27, 2020

I'm so proud of my daughter, Tiffany,
who's going to be another asset,
even if she doesn't manage her weight
as she should. But what a speech. I'm happy
she could join the rest of the family,
all taking their impressive turns. What great
talents — amazing how they communicate
their love and devotion. I have pretty
daughters, handsome sons, and a beautiful,
loving wife who still looks like a model
despite being a mother. They're awful,
the fake lamestream and their little puddle
of hate. I'm keeping America great.
Tiffany's the new Ivanka. She's great!

August 28, 2020

Never has a decision been clearer.
Old Sleepy Joe Biden is a corrupt
career politician who will make up
stories and outright lies. He's about fear
and defunding our brave police. I'm here
doing the job perfectly: Donald Trump
demands law and order. He's not a lump
in a basement like Joe Biden. I'm here
to promise we'll put the Deep State traitors
in jail, all of them, including Crooked
Hillary, and Biden's operator,
Obama. Their wallets and pocketbooks
are filled with what they took from our country.
Only Donald Trump can save this country!

August 29, 2020

I love Louisiana and Texas.
The hurricane is so unfortunate —
tough wind and rain in two wonderful states.
We've been hit at Mar-a-Lago — a mess
for weeks. Doral, too. They'll do fine unless
they start coming to me with their hands out
for extra money. Please, no more about
FEMA aid. The governor of Texas
is a real success story. He gets to
look up to me from his chair. Also true —
Louisiana's Democrat is so
weak. He completely botched the Chinese flu.
His state is Republican, but he's not.
I saw flooding. They'll get through it. Or not.

August 30, 2020

They always say I can't do what I do.
Donald Trump doesn't play by the same rules
as the others. Such dopey leftist fools,
the Democrats. Some Republicans, too,
are just stupid losers. I'll name a few —
Jeff Sessions and Mittens Romney. All schools
have got to reopen. It's very cruel
some colleges canceled sports. If they knew
what I knew, they'd play again tomorrow.
Football is the best. Basketball, the worst.
The pros make sneaky millions we all know
they don't earn. Players and coaches should first
shut up and play! I've made the White House home.
I'll do what it takes to defend my home.

August 31, 2020

I'm flying to Kenosha, Wisconsin
tomorrow to deal with the mobs and fear
taking over the country. You won't hear
Old Sleepy Joe talk of this. If he wins,
it's rigged, and protests will surge. If I win,
I promise it won't take me a half year
to beat the radical looters and queers
rioting in the streets. I have to win
so we'll achieve perfect law and order,
and continue successful policies.
You all see what I've done at the border —
my beautiful wall is rising. I'll quickly
finish it. No migrants! No protesters!
No Antifa! We'll handle protesters!

III

September 1, 2020

The governor of Wisconsin and mayor
of Kenosha are traitors. Presidents
should always be most welcome. Their nonsense
is what's causing riots, and they don't care.
I'd love to throw them in their own jails where
they belong. Socialist traitors! Events
like mine are a celebration against
the leftist agenda. Today I dare
to go where others fear. My job demands
upholding law and order no matter
what. As Commander in Chief here I stand.
Protesters must be dealt with. The squatters
and looters sicken me. Thugs! Arrest them
all. Criminals, every last one of them.

September 2, 2020

Old Man Sleepy Joe ought to be ashamed —
he's acting worse by the day. He refused
health tests and we know why. I think he'd choose
to spend the rest of his life downstairs chained
to his basement bed. They're saying he's blamed
his lies on a series of strokes. He used
to be very smart, but his one excuse
is he's senile so he forgets his own name
sometimes. Someone with his problems can't fight
the rioters and looters. Some are in
planes flying to cities during the night
to join protesters. It's violation
after violation. Old Sleepy Joe
hates God, too. He's finished, Old Sleepy Joe.

September 3, 2020

The CDC is the worst agency —
for a year they've been using bad numbers
to count deaths. I call them dumb and dumber,
since they should just count those who are healthy
who die of this. It's a great big fancy
cover-up they have going. This summer
I figured it out. Dishonest numbers!
I've learned six per cent is who are really
dying from the Chinese flu. Six per cent!
It's not however-many-thousand dead —
it's maybe ten thousand total. We went
through the complete statistics. They cheated
and the Deep State keeps trying to cheat. No
one is dying from this. That's what I know.

September 4, 2020

Very big months coming up. Very big.
Democrat-led cities are rioting.
Before our eyes they're disintegrating,
and all the lamestream wants is to help rig
the election. It's very, very big
business, the fake news, exaggerating
radicals' support. We see the fighting
and looting everywhere. Socialist pigs
are trying to steal the country. They say
I don't honor our brave military.
I *love* the men and women who have stayed
the course and served. Living vets are very
good people. If they have to mail in votes,
they should also go in person and vote.

September 5, 2020

Nobody tells Donald Trump what to do
since he's the most popular president
in history with one hundred per cent
enthusiasm from the very true
patriots who support him. They don't screw
around, my supporters. They're not violent,
but they all love the Second Amendment
so are armed and ready. They have great views
of right and wrong. Unlike Michael Cohen
who deserves to be shot, or jailed for life.
Give him a chance to flip, he'd sell his own
family to Muslims. I hear his wife
is divorcing him for his book money.
Trump's even more popular than money.

September 6, 2020

We really need to close down those outlets
like *The New York Times* and *Washington Post.*
Also CNN. Fake news is the most
harmful threat to our way of life. I'd bet
they'd all be losing more money except
for my popularity. I'm the most
important person in the world, and host
important foreign leaders. Don't forget
that Obama tried his best to bankrupt
our great country. He and Old Sleepy Joe
spied on me, breaking every law. Corrupt
as could be. Corrupt! But you'd never know
from the lamestream. We've got to shut it down,
then lock up Obama. He's going down.

September 7, 2020

The fake news is running wild all over
and has gotten worse. They like protesters
and always take their side. The protesters
are peaceful, they say, since they don't cover
what's really happening. We'll recover
when we send troops to round up protesters.
These are the worst people, the protesters.
They loot, they steal, they hate. And how they love
to set fire and burn down their own cities.
Socialist Democratic radicals
will burn the whole West Coast. It's not pretty
what they do. It's very despicable.
I never said what fake news said I said.
I never said it! They don't know what I said!

Postscript

September 11, 2020

I'm doing what it takes to continue
being your most popular president.
Melania is the most elegant
first lady in history. She can do
anything with design. Whatever's new
is her specialty. The money she's spent
always gets returns. I love the events
she produced for me. We can't have too
many dinners and fundraisers. We look
to win big in November. A landslide
that will destroy Old Sleepy Joe, a crook
if I've ever seen one. Old Joe Biden
will be retired at last with no mercy.
Today's a major anniversary.

September 14, 2020

Maybe the fraud, Woodward, got me on tape.
So what? If the virus was bad as claimed,
he'd have written his story then. He blames
everyone but himself. He'd call it rape
if he got another big headline. Tapes?
Who the hell cares! Everyone knows my name—
the greatest president who ever came
to the White House. We've made it ours. New drapes,
new rose garden, new fence. We plan to live
there for the rest of my life. People love
me for who I am. Everyday I give
them more of me. Tapes? I'm so far above
a hack like Bob Woodward. A petty crook
faking the whole thing to sell a few books.

September 20, 2020

She was not my type of female, the judge,
but we always treated her cordially.
Very small. Often sick. The vacancy
has got to be filled — Mitch and I won't budge
on that. It's incredible there's so much
talk of her. It's me making history
every day. This election allows me
four more years at least to drain the thick sludge
of swamp that's drowning Washington. Frankly,
the court has been at the center of this
liberal take-over. No, I'm not sorry,
since we've got to get down to business
these weeks. I want this pick very badly,
and I'll get it over her dead body.

September 24, 2020

I know the law better than the lawyers.
The Democrats have no chance, as in none,
unless they cheat. The voting will be done
when I say it's done, and that's an order.
If a judge disagrees, there's another
who'll see it my way. It only takes one
ruling, and the Supreme Court's great function
is to make final decisions. Lawyers
can't believe how I know every last thing
about law. That's how I've been the best
president in history. I'm planning
to live inside the White House for the rest
of my life. Melania and I will
redesign the space. It's way too little.

September 30, 2020

Fake news. How often do I have to say
fake news? The failed *New York Times* doesn't have
tax information. I love troops—and gave
extra support to the military
that Obama slandered. I was very
smart last night in debate, and very brave
to go after Old Sleepy Joe, who caved
from the start. Basement loser! He can't play
this game. I think it was my finest show
ever—huge ratings. Old Sleepy Joe looked
lost without his mask. Weakling with below
minus personality and crooked
son. I'm feeling a bit feverish here
today. Not myself. Someone do my hair!

Other works by Ken Waldman

Poetry and Prose:
Trump Sonnets, Volume 6 (Ridgeway Press, 2021)
Trump Sonnets, Volume 5 (Ridgeway Press, 2021)
The Writing Party (Mezcalita Press, 2020)
Sports Page (Lamar University Literary Press, 2020)
Trump Sonnets, Volume 4 (Ridgeway Press, 2020)
Trump Sonnets, Volume 3 (Ridgeway Press, 2019)
Trump Sonnets, Volume 2 (Ridgeway Press, 2018)
Trump Sonnets, Volume 1 (Ridgeway Press, 2017)
D is for Dog Team (Nomadic Press children's book, 2009)
Are You Famous? (Catalyst Book Press, 2008)
As the World Burns (Ridgeway Press, 2006)
Conditions and Cures (Steel Toe Books, 2006)
And Shadow Remained (Pavement Saw Press, 2006)
The Secret Visitor's Guide (Wings Press, 2006)
To Live on This Earth (West End Press, 2002)
Nome Poems (West End Press, 2000)

Recordings:
D is for Dog Team (Nomadic Press, 2009)
Some Favorites (Nomadic Press, 2009)
55 Tunes, 5 Poems (Nomadic Press, 2008)
As the World Burns (Nomadic Press, 2006)
All Originals, All Traditionals (Nomadic Press, 2006)
Fiddling Poets on Parade (Nomadic Press, 2006)
Music Party (Nomadic Press, 2003)
Burnt Down House (Nomadic Press, 2001)
A Week in Eek (Nomadic Press, 2000)